The New Adventures of Postman Pat

Postman Pat™

and the robot

John Cunliffe

Illustrated by Stuart Trotter

from the original television designs by Ivor Wood

a division of Hodder Headline plc

More Postman Pat adventures:

Postman Pat in a muddle
Postman Pat misses the show
Postman Pat follows a trail
Postman Pat and the hole in the road
Postman Pat and the suit of armour
Postman Pat has the best village
Postman Pat has a big surprise
Postman Pat paints the ceiling
Postman Pat has too many parcels
Postman Pat takes flight

First published in hardback 1997
This paperback edition published 1997

ISBN 0 340 70915 4
10 9 8 7 6 5 4 3 2 1

A catalogue record for this book is available
from the British Library.

Printed in Italy.

Hodder Children's Books,
a division of Hodder Headline plc,
338 Euston Road, London NW1 3BH

“I’m so tired,” said Pat. “I feel too tired to take the post.”
“Go and see the doctor,” said Sara.
So he did.

Doctor Gilbertson listened to Pat's heart; she tapped his knee; she took his temperature.

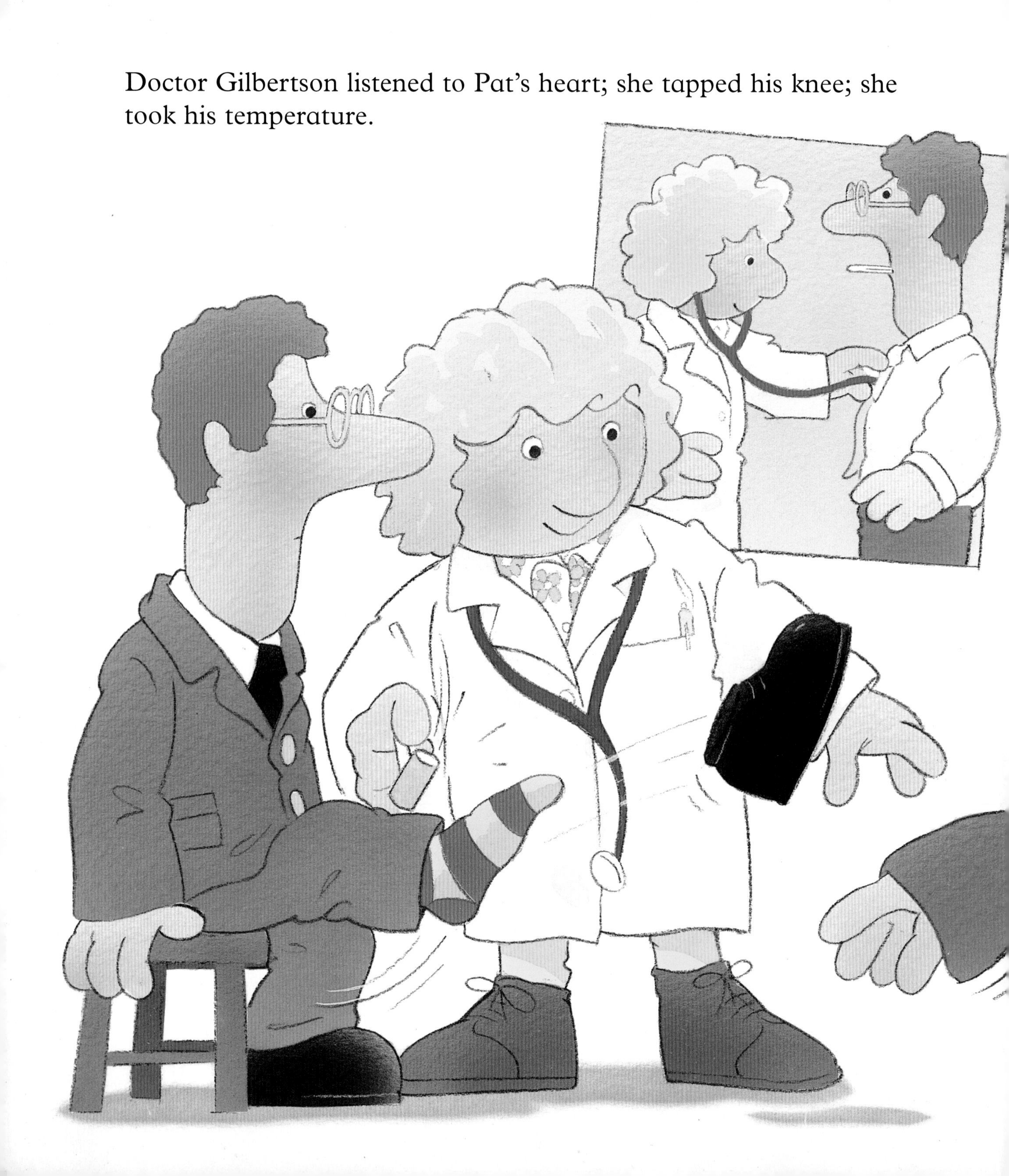

"There's nothing wrong with you," she said. "I'll give you some vitamins - a wee tonic - you're a bit run down. Working too hard?"

"Well," said Pat, "there *is* a lot of post these days."

"Now don't you be overdoing it, Pat. Just take it steady," said Doctor Gilbertson. "You'll be fine if you just have a rest sometimes."

"Thanks," said Pat. "Cheerio, Doctor!"

With being so tired, and going to see the doctor, Pat was late arriving at the Post Office.

"Morning, Mrs Goggins!" he yawned. "Oh, dear, I'm so sleepy! Sorry I'm so late . . . I popped in to see Doctor Gilbertson . . . I thought she might give me something to keep me going . . ."

"Oh, Pat," said Mrs Goggins, "I'm sorry you're feeling so poorly . . . what with all this post waiting to be delivered and so many parcels . . ."

"I could go to sleep right now," said Pat. "Never mind, I'd better be on my way! Bye! Lucky old Jess! It must be nice being a cat, snoozing all day in the sun!"

Pat went . . . slowly . . . on his way.

Greendale itself seemed sleepy, today. But not in Ted Glen's workshop! Not a bit of it! Something was clicking, and whirring, and beeping, all day and half the night! What was happening?

Pat stopped to investigate.

"Morning, Pat!" said Ted. "Sorry, can't stop!"

"No wonder there's a lot of post to deliver! All these boxes! Whatever are you up to, Ted?"

"Come and have a look at this!" said Ted. "It's a right bobby dazzler! Can you pass a box of that paper?"

"Is this it? Oooops!"

"That's right, Pat. You bung it in this printer, and then plug it into the computer, and off you go!"

"Where?"

"Anywhere you like!" laughed Ted.

"This looks like spaghetti-junction! What does it do?" said Pat.

"Nay, Pat, it's a drawing for a new invention. You can do it at a rate of knots on the computer - not like pencil-and-paper - it keeps going while I'm asleep."

"Sounds all right to me," said Pat. "Do you think it could deliver letters, while *I'm* asleep?"

"A robot, that's what you need for that, Pat. Look at this book ! It tells you how to make them . . . *No job too difficult*, it says!"

"A robot postman? Could you make one?" said Pat.

"I reckon I could. You can do anything with a computer. Take a day or two, mind."

"Then I could have a day off?"

"You could have a week off! It could deliver all your letters and parcels in ten minutes flat. Have a look at this, now. I'll print it out for you, then you can take it to show Sara and Julian."

A robot danced across the screen.
"Bless us all!" shouted Pat. "Robots . . . coming to life! Hey up! What next?"

Paper began to spew out of Ted's printer, more and more of it, rolling across the floor, and wrapping itself round Pat's legs.

"Now, then . . . don't worry . . ." said Ted, "I'll just . . . now which key do you press to stop it? Oh help!"

"I think it's trying to get me!" said Pat, backing out of the door. "I'll pop in when you've got it sorted out! There's a letter for you somewhere under that lot! Bye, Ted!"

"Oh, help! Pat?" yelled Ted. "Come back! Help!"

A few days after that, Mrs Goggins heard a sound in the post-office, and, when she went to see what it was, a strange thing glared over the counter at her.

"Oh! Gracious me! What is it? Shoo!" she screamed.

She waved her broom at it.

"One step nearer and you get this in your sprockets! Off with you! Shoo!"

Ted Glen bobbed up beside it, twiddling with its knobs.

"It's all right, Mrs Goggins, don't sweep us out! It's only the new robot postman - it'll give Pat a good rest. It's out for its test-run. Just give it a load of post, and it'll be gone in no time. It *never* gets tired."

"Well, I don't know about trusting the mail to such a contraption," said Mrs Goggins, "I'd rather have our Pat."

"There's no need to worry at all. It's all worked by a computer. Can't go wrong . . . all I have to do is to program it properly, and off it goes. There you are! It can't wait to be on its way! Ta-ta, robot!"

The robot crashed into the wall.

"Oh . . . it needs a slight adjustment . . ."

"Hmm, just what I supposed. I've heard about these computers . . ." said Mrs Goggins.

"It only wants fettling," said Ted. "Sorting out a bit, here and there. . ."

"Well, *I'll* sort the letters out," said Mrs Goggins. "That should help it."

Ted threw a switch. There was a blue flash.

"Power on! Hey up! Look out, it's off! Whoa, Dobbin!"

The robot swiped all the letters off the counter before Mrs Goggins could sort them, and off it went, at top speed.

"There's no stopping it now!" shouted Ted, as he ran after it. "I'll just keep an eye on it . . ."

Pat had finished the first lot of post, and was coming back for more, when he met Ted.

"Have you seen that robot, Pat?" Ted gasped. "It's gone off with the rest of the post!"

"I thought I heard a funny noise!" said Pat. "Look - follow the trail of letters!"

"Don't worry, I'll soon put it right," said Ted.

Soon, they met the Reverend Timms. He looked very upset about something.

"Oh, Pat, Ted, a most dreadful thing - a - a - well, it looked like a monster - a tin monster - and it rushed up to me, and thrust all these letters into my hand, and not one of them is for me!"

"We're just sorting things out, Reverend, don't worry!" said Ted.

More shouts and yells came round the next corner, followed by Miss Hubbard and Peter Fogg, at the run. The robot was chasing them, with huge bundles of letters. They all hid behind dustbins and plant-pots, and the robot stopped, wondering who to give the letters to.

Ted crept up behind it. "Now then, I'll just switch you off, and. . ."

But the robot whirled round
and tried to stuff a letter into his mouth.
"Oh! It's not for me, you idiot!
And . . . you're supposed to put them in letter-boxes!"
The robot didn't stop to listen. Off it went, looking for more victims.

"Come back!" Ted shouted. "Oh, dear, it's not programmed to come back . . ."

"It's going too fast for us," said Pat. "Why don't we go after it in the post-bus?"

"Good idea!" said Ted. "Get a move on, Pat!"

They ran for the bus. Off they went, as fast as they could.

They met Sam Waldron, with his van stuck in a field-gate.

"Whatever's happened to your van, Sam?" said Pat.

"It was an alien from outer space," said Sam. "It came belting down that road - I went straight into the field to dodge it!"

"Which way did it go?" said Ted.

"I think it was heading for Thompson Ground."

"Let's take a short-cut across the field," said Pat. "We might be able to cut it off before it gets there."

They arrived at Thompson Ground the back way.
"Come on," said Ted. "I think the robot's beaten us to it . . ."

Dorothy had no idea what was going on in her barn. Something was blundering about, giving letters to the hens. Then it shot out, got all mixed up in the line of washing, thrust a letter into Dorothy's apron-pocket, and whizzed off across a field of turnips. Alf came out, to see what was going on.

"What in the world was that?" said Dorothy.

As they all watched, the robot got more and more bogged down in the mud. In the middle of the field, it stuck fast, with its arms still waving, and its lights flashing.

"I'm sorry about all this," said Ted. "I'll explain later. Just let me take it away, and break it up for spare parts . . ."

"Nay, leave it," said Alf. "It makes a grand scarecrow. I've been having a lot of bother with these crows, and look - it's scared them off, every single one of them!"

The robot seemed to like being a scarecrow.

When the other Greendale farmers heard about Alf and Dorothy's wonderful new electric scarecrow, they all wanted one. Ted was kept busy making robot-scarecrows for a long time after that.

It was bad news for the crows, though!